Me and the Eggman

Me and the Eggman

by ELEANOR CLYMER

illustrated by David K. Stone

E. P. DUTTON & CO., INC. NEW YORK

Other Books by Eleanor Clymer

The Big Pile of Dirt
The House on the Mountain
My Brother Stevie
The Second Greatest Invention
We Lived in the Almont

Published simultaneously in Canada by Clarke,
Irwin & Company Limited, Toronto and Vancouver

SBN: 0-525-34775-5   LCC: 75-179054

Designed by Hilda Scott
Printed in the U.S.A.
First Edition

For Deirdre

one

I used to sit around a lot and imagine things. I'd think about all the great things I would like to do, like be a racing driver, or find a whole lot of money, or catch a criminal. It didn't make much sense, but I did it anyhow. I'd watch TV and get all these crazy ideas. Then I got to know the Eggman. Now I have something to think about that I don't have to imagine. It's real.

It happened last summer. It started with John. He's my brother. He's ten years older than me. We used to have a lot of fun together. He would go out with me and play ball, or he'd help me make models. We'd go for walks and he'd explain things to me. If we met his friends he'd say, This is my kid brother Donald. And he would muss up my hair so they could see he liked me.

Then he went to the Army. I thought he looked great in his uniform. Mom didn't like it. She wanted him to try to get into some college. But John said, Let's face it, Mom, we haven't got the money for college. I'll learn just as much in the Army. So he went.

I missed him. Right after he left I couldn't sleep and I almost didn't want to eat. I could hardly wait for him to come back. Then last fall he came back and he was different. It did something to him. I don't know what it was, but he acted sore all the time.

He got mad at the little kids, Julie and Douglas, when they made a noise. He argued with my sister Mary. If Mom called him for supper, he'd say, All right, all right, I heard you, I'm not deaf. Nobody could say a thing to him.

But it was worst for me. He had no time for me at all. He yelled at me sometimes for not helping Mom. But mostly he hardly even saw me. I'd talk to him and say, Hey, John, what did you do in the Army? He wouldn't even answer. I'd say, You want to go out and have a catch? He'd say, No, not now.

I felt like saying, Hey, it's me, Donald. Remember me? I didn't have a lot of friends the way some kids do, so I could hardly wait for him to get home, thinking of all the things we'd do together. And then he was like a stranger.

He had a job in a garage, fixing cars. He learned that in the Army. And he went to school a couple of nights a week, he was taking a course about motors. But the rest of the time he watched TV, or he'd go out.

He didn't like the place we lived in. It was the same

place we had before he went away, but now he griped about it. Well, I guess it isn't too good. It's on the top floor, hot in summer and cold in winter. And we don't have too much room. Somebody has to sleep in every room. If you watched TV it would wake up the kids, or if John was out late and wanted to sleep in the morning, we would make noise and wake him up.

Mom said, Children, please keep quiet. You're bothering your brother.

I said, We weren't doing anything.

John said, The heck with it. I go away and knock myself out and come back to a place like this.

3

Mom said, It's the best we can do.

John said, It's not good enough. We have to do something about it.

Mom couldn't do anything about it except ask me and the kids to please not annoy our brother.

I said, What's the matter? What did we do?

Mom said, You didn't do anything. He's in a bad mood since he came back.

My sister Mary said, Maybe it's his girl friend.

He had this girl he used to go with, and now she goes with somebody else. I didn't know why that should make him yell at *us*. Mom said, No. It was the Army that did it to him.

It wasn't so easy to stay out of his way. In the winter we had to stay in the house a lot. I thought that when summer came I'd be able to get out. I could hardly wait for school to be over. I hated school. It was so boring, sitting inside four walls all the time. When spring came, I'd cut school sometimes and go over to the river. I knew I could get in trouble, but I did it anyhow. It was worth it, only when Mom found out she felt bad, and when John found out he'd yell at me. Also it was lonesome.

So I thought, When summer comes maybe some of the kids will ask me to go places with them, go to the beach or the park.

Then, just when school was almost over, there was a problem. Mom was going to send the little kids to a day-care center. But the center was full and there was no place for them. The lady said maybe later in the summer there would be room.

So what to do with the kids?

We had a neighbor who always minded them after school. Mom asked her if she could take them, but she was moving. So there was nobody to mind the kids.

We were eating supper and talking about it. I remember it was warm and the windows were open, we could hear the traffic and the kids shouting in the street.

Mom said, I don't know what to do. Maybe I'll have to stop working and go on welfare.

Mary said, No. I'll stay home. My job isn't so important. (Mary had a baby-sitting job for the summer.)

But Mom wouldn't let her. Mary was saving up to go to college. Mom said, At least one person in this family is going to go.

That made John mad because it was like saying he should have gone. So of course he had to take it out on me.

He said, Why can't Donald mind the kids? He's big enough.

Mom looked as if she didn't think so. I didn't think so either. She said, Well, for a day or two, but not all summer.

John asked, Why not?

Mom answered, Well, you know they're always into something.

It's true. They don't do anything bad, but you never

know. Like Douglas is always bringing home cats. One time he brought this cat that had fleas. Boy, we had fleas all over the house.

Mom said, You get rid of that cat. So he and Julie took it on the roof and it ran away. But while they were up there they found this tub full of dirt, so they made a garden. They planted beans. Douglas learned how to do it in school. They took water up there and watered the beans till the water ran through the ceiling. Those kids need somebody to watch them.

Mom said, I wish they could go to Aunt Lizzie. All of them.

Aunt Lizzie is Mom's aunt, and Mom used to live with her when she was little. She told us how nice it was, way out in the country, where you didn't have to wear shoes and could climb trees and pick berries and that. She also told us how strict Aunt Lizzie was, how she'd never let you eat pie till you cleaned your plate, or play before you did your chores, or go to bed without washing your feet. So I wasn't crazy to go there.

Aunt Lizzie was always writing to Mom to ask her to come for a visit because she was getting old and wanted to see her before she died. Mom didn't have the money or the time to go, and she would write back and ask Aunt Lizzie to come see us, but she never would. She said she wanted to die in her own place and not in some big city where nobody cared about her.

Mom didn't mean it about sending us to Aunt Lizzie

and I was glad. But what were we going to do?

Then a few days later we had a surprise. Mom got a letter from Aunt Lizzie, and she wanted to come and see *us*! She said there had been a bad storm and her house got flooded, her garden was ruined, and her cow was dead, and she was too old to start again. She was living with some neighbors but they had six children and four grandchildren, so she couldn't stay there. She wanted to come and see us before she died.

Mom said, Maybe this is the answer to our prayers. Of course she may not stay long, she won't like the city. And I know she's not strong. But maybe she can just keep an eye on the children for a few weeks, till the center has room for them.

It seemed like a good idea.

Mom kept reminding us, Remember, she is old and weak and can't do much, and it will be crowded. We said we'd do all the work, and we'd keep quiet so as not to bother her, and we'd try not to get in the way. I thought it wouldn't matter to me, because if Aunt Lizzie was there, I could be out most of the time.

That's what I thought till she arrived.

We spent a whole weekend getting ready for her. Mary and Mom cleaned the house and we moved furniture so she could share a bedroom with Julie. Then Mom and John went to the bus to meet her and the rest of us waited, wondering if she would be able to climb the stairs, weak and old as she was. Well, that was a laugh.

She was old, all right. A tiny little woman with white hair and wrinkles. But not weak. At least she wouldn't admit it.

She looked at us all and said we favored Mom, and then she said, Well, Sarah, what you want I should do?

Mom said, Aunt Lizzie, you're not going to do a thing. We'll have supper and then you're going to rest.

She said, Rest! I'm not tired, I've been sitting on that bus all day doing nothing.

We had a good dinner, chicken and mashed potatoes and a pie from the store. Aunt Lizzie didn't eat the crust.

She said, Sarah, I guess you don't get to do much baking. She did go to bed early. And she was up early, too. Mary was going to stay home from her job for a few days, but Aunt Lizzie said, You don't need to. I can mind the house.

So Mom said, Now, Donald, you help Aunt Lizzie and don't let her work. Then they left.

As soon as they were gone, Aunt Lizzie said, Donald, get me a bucket of water and a brush. And she started cleaning house. I told her Mom cleaned yesterday, but it didn't suit her. She had to do it all over again and I had to help. Even Julie and Douglas helped. We scrubbed the bathroom and mopped the kitchen.

When the house was clean enough for her, she sent me to the store to get raisins and flour and stuff to bake with. She made cookies and pie. I had to admit they were good. I could see why she didn't eat the store-bought pie.

When Mom and Mary got home they made a big fuss because the house was so clean and the dinner was all ready, but they said they didn't want her to work. She said, It was nothing. Donald helped me.

So they looked at me real pleased. What could I say? I just hoped she'd get tired of cleaning after a while.

But she didn't. She was crazy about it. She kept after me all the time to help. And she thought she was supposed to baby-sit me as well as the kids! If I tried to sneak out, she'd call after me, Donald! Where are you going? Take Julie and Douglas with you and come back soon, hear?

I had to take the wash to the laundromat nearly every day. I'd meet kids I knew and they'd laugh and yell, Poor Donald, he has to work.

Work! We washed the windows and then she decided to wash the walls. I thought, If she gets up on a chair and falls off, Mom will blame me. So I did it.

Mom said, Aunt Lizzie, why can't you take it easy?

She said, I got to have something to do, and besides, I don't want to be a burden to you, Sarah. As long as I'm here I'm going to earn my board and keep. Just because I'm old doesn't mean I'm ready for the junk pile.

Mom said, Of course not, Aunt Lizzie, but you don't have to work so hard.

Aunt Lizzie said, What's so hard? There's no outside work. Now if I had my chickens and my cow, I might be a little tired. But all you got here is roaches. Ugh!

She sure did hate those roaches. If one roach showed

its head she was after it with the broom. The place was so clean, though, the roaches just about starved to death.

The worst thing was that it was so crowded. There were beds in all the rooms except the kitchen. You could hardly move. It must be like that in jail.

I thought, I have to get out of here. So one time when Aunt Lizzie sent me out for groceries, with the kids tagging along, I gave them each a quarter and told them to buy candy and go home. Then I went over to the river and stayed all day. I bought food and ate it. But it wasn't any fun because I was so mad, and besides, I felt bad about running out.

When I got back Mom was home and she gave me Hail Columbia. I thought at least John would understand, but he yelled at me and said I had no consideration. The next day I had to stay in the house all day and I was so mad I didn't talk to anybody, and if the kids bothered me I smacked them.

I started to think I'd like to leave for good. I wondered where I could go. Then I had an idea.

There was this old man who used to come every Wednesday with eggs and vegetables. He had been coming for a long time and I never paid much attention, but Aunt Lizzie wanted to know all about him. She started asking him a lot of questions.

He told her he had a farm in the country somewhere, with a cow and chickens and a garden. He used to sell eggs to a boardinghouse but it closed, so now he came to the city once a week. He looked mad when she asked him things. He didn't like to talk, but she wouldn't pay him till she got through talking, so he had to stand there and wait.

He'd say, Come on, lady, I got a long drive home, I got to take care of the cow and feed the chickens.

She asked, Don't you have anybody to help you?

He said, No. What do I need help for?

She asked him, Well, haven't you got anybody to wash your clothes and that? (He wore overalls and looked pretty dirty.)

He said, Don't need nobody. I had a wife but she died. I get along by myself.

Aunt Lizzie asked him if he had neighbors, and he said, Yes, but I don't bother them and they don't bother me. Got no use for nosy people. Always bossing you.

I thought, You're right, man.

Aunt Lizzie asked what he did with the cow's milk. He said, Some the neighbors take and some I give to the cat. Right now, cow's dry. Going to have a calf soon.

When Mom got home Douglas said, I want to go and see the Eggman. He's got a cow. And a cat. I want to see the cat. Maybe he'd give it to me.

Mom said, Douglas, keep still, you can't go there.

That gave me an idea. I thought, Maybe *I* can go there. I had a picture in my mind of what a farm was like. When I was in the third grade we had this social studies book with pictures of a farm. There was a white house with a flower garden, and a red barn, and horses and cows, and the mother was always wearing a clean dress, and always cooking and smiling. And the father rode on a tractor and milked the cows with a machine and the kids helped. They had a dog and a cat and a pony.

Well, I thought the Eggman's place must be something like that. I thought, Maybe he'll let me go and do the farm work. The next time he comes I'll ask him. I'll say, Mister, you want a boy to help you? I'm strong, and you don't have to pay me. I'll ask him next Wednesday.

So I waited and waited, and I began to get scared. I didn't think I'd have the nerve to ask him. Even if I did, he wouldn't want me. It was a crazy idea.

Then I thought, If John would talk to me, I'd stay.

So Tuesday night after supper I said, Hey, you want to take a walk with me?

But he said, No. I'm too tired. You know I work all day. I don't just play around.

So I thought, That's it. I'll get out.

So when Wednesday came, I waited in the street and when I saw the Eggman's truck coming, I hid. I watched him get out of the cab and go to the back. He opened the door and took out his basket. Then he went inside the house.

I went to the back of the truck and opened the door. There were some old quilts in there, and some empty baskets. I felt very scared at what I was doing. It was almost as if it was another person doing it and me watching, thinking, That guy is crazy.

I climbed inside the truck and banged the door shut.

It was dark in there. I thought, What a dopey thing to do! Then I decided, This is dumb. I'd better get out of here.

I pushed the door, but it wouldn't open. I was trapped!

Now what was I going to do? I banged on the door and yelled, but nobody heard me. I thought, Well, the old man will be back soon. So I sat on the quilts and waited. He was taking a long time. I thought Aunt Lizzie must be talking his ear off. Then I heard him. I thought he would open the back to put his basket in, but he didn't. He just climbed up and started the motor.

The next thing I knew, the truck was moving. I thought, I ought to yell and bang, but I was scared to. I might frighten the Eggman and he might have an accident. Then I decided, as long as I've come this far, I might as well wait and see what happens.

I was scared, but I couldn't go back.

two

The truck kept on going for a long time. It bumped and rattled something awful. It was a pretty old truck and didn't have good springs. I was getting dizzy from all that jolting. Maybe I dozed off for a while, I don't remember. At last we stopped.

I couldn't see or hear a thing. I yelled, Hey! and banged on the side of the truck. The door opened and I looked out.

It was dark, and there were red and blue lights. We were at a gas station. It was raining. The Eggman was staring at me with his mouth open.

Then he said, What in the Sam Hill are you doing here?

I said, Well, I got in the truck and then I couldn't get out.

He said, Couldn't you yell?

I told him, I did but you didn't hear me.

He said, Well, what am I gonna do with you now?

I asked, Couldn't I go with you?

I wanted to tell him how strong I was, and all, but this wasn't the right time for it.

He said, You want to get me in trouble? What about your folks? They're probably going crazy looking for you.

I said, I didn't think of that.

He was getting madder every second. He yelled, You didn't think! Haven't you got any brains?

We were getting soaked. The gas station man, too. He said, Come on inside and talk about this.

So we went inside and the Eggman said, I guess you better phone your folks. You can phone from here. I haven't got any phone in my house. And hurry up. My cow's out in the rain. I got to get home.

The gas station man said, You better phone collect. What's your number? I'll get it for you.

So I told him and the next thing I was saying, Hello, this is Donald.

Just my luck, John was on the phone. He shouted at me, Donald, where are you? When I told him, he was so mad he almost broke the phone. He said, We were looking all over the neighborhood for you. Wait till I get hold of you.

I said, I couldn't help it. (It wasn't much use telling him why I did it.)

He said, Let me talk to the Eggman.

The Eggman got on the phone and said he wasn't planning to go back to the city till next Wednesday, so John said, Well, will you keep him there till then? We'll pay you. (I could hear because he was shouting so loud.)

The Eggman said, I don't want no pay. I don't want him either, it wasn't my idea.

Then he hung up.

We got back in the truck, and this time he let me sit in front with him. The road was black and shiny in the rain, and the headlights made a bright reflection in the blackness. I was cold and hungry, but most of all I wished he wouldn't be so mad at me.

I said, I won't be in your way. I can work. I'm strong.

He didn't say anything.

We went about a mile from the gas station and then we turned off into a side road. It was a dirt road, very bumpy, with trees on both sides. We went a couple of miles, mostly uphill, and then turned off and stopped.

The Eggman got down and said, Come on. He started walking and I followed him. I could hardly see where I was going, and I stumbled over rocks in the path and almost fell on my face in a puddle. Then I saw a house. A dog on the porch barked.

The Eggman said, Shut up. He walked in and I followed him.

It was pitch dark. I bumped into something. I wondered why he didn't switch on the light. But instead he struck a match and lit a kerosene lamp on the table. I found out later he didn't have any electricity. I looked around, and was I surprised! I thought I would see a nice place, all white and clean. Instead of that it was dark and messy. There was a stove and a table and chairs, and a couch in the corner. Dirty dishes were on the table, old rags and junk on the floor.

I was starved. But the Eggman didn't do anything about eating. He lit a lantern and said, Got to make sure the cow's all right. I left her in the lot behind the barn. You can wait here.

I didn't want to stay by myself, so I asked, Can I go with you?

He said, Well, come on.

We went out and walked through a lot of mud. He seemed to know where he was going. I sure didn't, but I kept up with him. The lantern made big spooky shadows in the darkness. I could see the barn ahead of us, but we didn't go in. We went around behind it. There was a kind of yard with a fence around it, but there was no cow there.

He said, Darn it, I left her in here but she got out. The bars are down. How the heck did that happen? She must be out in the pasture.

We went out to a field. In the middle of the field was a tree, and he headed for it. There she was, a big black shape.

She said, *Mooo!* Then I saw something else. On the ground next to her was a black lump.

The Eggman began to swear.

I said, What's the matter?

He said, She had her calf out here in the field. Now we got to get it to the barn.

He went over to it and poked it and tried to make it stand up, but it wouldn't.

He said, I guess I'll have to carry it. You help me.

He bent down and we heaved and pulled and finally we got it on to his shoulders. It was wet and slippery and hard to get hold of. Then I held the lantern and we made it to the barn. The cow followed us. We put the calf down in a stall and the Eggman took some rags and said, Here, we got to rub it and get it dry and warm.

So we rubbed. The cow watched. After a while the Eggman said, Take a bucket and get some water for the cow.

I didn't see any bucket, and I didn't see any water, so he said, Over there, the pump! The pump!

I still didn't know what to do, and he got real mad and said, You don't know much, do you?

But he got the water himself and gave the cow a drink. Then he gave her some feed, and then he rubbed some more, and the calf opened its eyes and tried to get on its feet. The cow tried to push it with her head and it fell down again.

I thought, You're a big help.

But finally the calf made it. It got up on all four feet and started to suck, and the cow licked its back.

I thought we were through, but we had more to do. We marched out in the darkness and mud and went to a kind of shed. It was the chicken house. We went in, and the chickens squawked and ran around till the Eggman threw some corn or something into a wooden thing for them to eat out of. Then I had to get water from the pump for them.

At last we went back to the house, and it was time for us to eat. The Eggman lit the stove and fried some eggs. He made coffee and cut some bread. Meantime the dog was making noises like he was hungry, too. He went outside the door and picked up a pan and dropped it on the floor in front of the Eggman. I thought that was pretty smart. The Eggman told him to shut up, but he gave him something to eat out of a bag. Some dry stuff that looked awful. The dog must have been awfully hungry, because he ate it.

Then the Eggman said to me, Here's some quilts. You can sleep on the couch. I'm going to bed.

And he went into the bedroom. He took the lamp with him. Some light came through the door, and I started fixing the quilts on the couch. Then I thought of something.

I said, Where's the bathroom?

He mumbled, What? Oh, I don't have no bathroom in the house. You can go outside.

So I went out. It wasn't raining any more. The moon was out, so I could see. The air smelled cool and good, and the trees dripped on me. But where was the bathroom?

Out back of the house was a little house, sort of like a wooden telephone booth. That was it. I knew because Aunt Lizzie had told us she had one. So I went in there. Then I went back to the house.

I was so tired I could hardly walk.

But I wasn't through yet. The Eggman called out, Did you shut the outhouse door? I can hear it banging. So I had to go back and shut it. Then I went to bed.

The dog climbed up and lay down next to me. I guess that was where he generally slept. He smelled pretty strong but he felt nice and warm. I was glad there was somebody around who wasn't mad.

When I woke up, I didn't know where I was. I was in a dirty kitchen, on a couch with springs poking me in the back, and something cold was poking my face. It was the dog's nose. Then I remembered. I was in the Eggman's house. It didn't look much better in the morning than it did at night. It looked worse because you could see more.

The Eggman was getting up. I could hear him groan as if something hurt him. He came out in the kitchen and made coffee.

I said, Hi. He just looked at me and grunted.

I asked, You want me to do anything?

He said, I got to do the chores first. You can help if you want. We drank some coffee and went out. Then I got a look at the place in daylight. No white house or red barn—just dirty gray. There were piles of junk all around, an old car, some broken chairs and old tires. No flower garden, just bare earth and mud, and a dead plant in a tin can. We went to the barn. The calf was all right. It was standing up and nursing.

The Eggman gave the cow some feed and water. Then we went to feed the chickens, and he told me to get the eggs.

I said, Where are they?

He said, In the nests. Where do you think they are? Go on. Take an empty bucket to put them in. Don't break them.

I went into the chicken house and looked for nests. There were some boxes nailed to the wall, and in one of them I saw an egg. So I took it. It was warm, and it felt nice and smooth. Then I looked for more. Pretty soon I had ten in the pail. The last nest had a chicken in it. She sat there looking at me as if she didn't like me. I thought, If there's an egg under her, how am I going to get it?

Just then she jumped off the nest right in my face, squawking her head off and flapping her wings. I shut

my eyes, and when I opened them she was gone and there was an egg there. I thought, Gee, she just laid it!

The Eggman was waiting for me. He didn't say thanks for getting the eggs. He said, Well, you took long enough. Now hook that door so they can't get out.

We went back to the house. He walked awfully stiff, and put his hand on his back. We had breakfast—eggs and bread and coffee again. I was wondering if there was ever anything else to eat.

Then he said, I have to go to the garden before it gets hot. You can come if you want.

He got a hoe and a basket from the back porch and we went to the garden. The gate was open. There was a rabbit inside eating some leaves. The Eggman chased it out. He said, What darn fool opened that gate?

There was lots of stuff growing there, corn and beans

and tomatoes. He told me to get down and pull some weeds. Of course he had to show me which were the weeds. Then he started to hoe the corn. But pretty soon he swore and stopped hoeing and put his hand on his back again.

Then he told me to pick some beans and put them in the basket. By the time I got half a basket I was pretty tired. Then he said to pick some tomatoes.

We went back to the house, me carrying the basket, which was pretty heavy, and the Eggman walking slow and stiff. He told me to put it down in the cellar, where it would keep cool, but first to take out some beans and tomatoes for our dinner. I was glad to hear we were going to eat. I snapped the beans and put them on to cook, and we had them and the tomatoes and a can of hash.

Then he said, I got to lie down for a while. And he went in the bedroom.

I sat there in the kitchen, thinking, This place is terrible. I was pretty dumb to come here, it isn't a bit like that farm in the social studies book. It's ugly and dirty and there's nothing good to eat, and anyhow the Eggman doesn't want me here. I thought, The way he bosses me around I'd be better off with Aunt Lizzie, at least she can cook. I didn't know if I could stand it till next Wednesday.

Anyhow I had to get out of that kitchen. I went out to the barn to look at the calf. It was real cute. It had that baby look. I wanted to pat it but I didn't know if the old cow would let me. She looked awfully big. But I put my hand out anyhow and rubbed the calf's head. It felt warm and hard, like a baseball with fur on it. The cow looked at me with her big eyes, and then she put out her tongue and licked my arm.

I saw her water bucket was empty, so I took it to the pump and filled it and she stuck her nose in and had a drink.

I went out in the sun and walked to the field. Just as I was going out of the barn I saw a yellow cat going in, with something in her mouth. I started after her but she ran away. I thought, Douglas would like that cat.

I went out in the field and sat under the tree. There was a brook running through the field. It was real quiet. There wasn't a sound except the water in the brook rippling, and a couple of birds flying around the tree. I felt peaceful. I lay down and looked up at the tree and the sky. I guess I fell asleep.

The next thing I knew, I was awake and the dog was sniffing at me. I patted him and talked to him. He was a nice dog.

I didn't know his name, so I said, I'll call you Blackie. (I never heard the Eggman call him anything except Shut up.) I got up and went back to the house.

The Eggman was mad. He said, Where did you go? What's the idea of going out without telling me?

I said, Well, I had nothing to do so I went out in the field.

He said, There's plenty to do here.

I said, Okay, tell me what to do.

He said, You could wash those dishes. (Looked like nobody had washed any dishes for a week.)

I asked him, Where's the sink?

He said, Use the dishpan.

Then I asked, Where's the soap and the dishcloth?

He said, You ask too many questions. And he lay down again.

I found a rag and a bar of soap, and I heated some water, and washed the dishes as well as I could. They didn't come out too clean. There was no towel, so I didn't dry them.

I swept the floor. I didn't know what to do with the dirt, so I threw it outside. I almost laughed when I thought what Aunt Lizzie would have to say about such housekeeping.

By that time the Eggman was up, and he said it was time to do the chores again. I thought, Gee, there's never any end to it. The minute you get through, it's time to start again.

We went to the barn, and he said the cow's stall needed cleaning. I could see that it did, but he said we would do it tomorrow. Then he told me to climb up in the loft and throw down some hay. While I was up there, I saw the yellow cat again, and she had two kittens. They sure were cute. I tried to catch one but it ran away and hid in the hay.

The Eggman hollered, Are you going to stay there all night? I threw down the hay and he threw it in the cow's stall and spread it around with the pitchfork.

We fed the chickens and went back to the house. We had supper. It wasn't much good, but I ate it anyhow because I was starved. Then there was nothing to do except go to bed again.

The couch was terrible. It sank down in the middle and the springs stuck into my back, and it wasn't really big enough for me and Blackie. So I got up my nerve and asked the old man if there was some other place I could sleep.

He said, Well, there's a room upstairs, but you'll have to take a candle. You better be careful and not burn the house down.

He lit a candle for me and I started upstairs. He called after me, Don't drop it, and blow it out before you get in bed.

At the top of the stairs there was a hall, and about four rooms opening from it. I didn't know the house was so big. I wondered which room he meant for me to sleep in, and then I saw that one was a boy's room. There were flags on the wall, and some model planes, and a baseball hat. It was a nice room. Everything was dusty, though, and the planes were old, not like the ones I had at home.

I put the candlestick on the table and got ready for bed. Then I blew it out. But before I got into bed I looked out of the window. The sky was dark blue, except there was one pinpoint of light. I thought it must be a plane but it didn't move, so I guessed it was a star.

three

The next morning when I woke up I won-
dered if the Eggman was feeling any better, so I went
down to his room. He was still in bed.

I asked him, Are you sick?

He groaned and said, It's my back. I put it out lifting
that calf. Come over here. Help me get up.

He took hold of my arm to pull himself up. I thought
my arm would break. I could see his back must be
hurting him, the way he swore. I thought if I felt that
bad I would stay in bed, but the place was such a
mess maybe it was better to get out of it. Also he had
a lot of work to do and it couldn't wait.

We had to go to the barn and let the cow out in
the field so she could eat grass and not have to be fed.
She was glad to get out, and the calf, too.

Then we had to clean out the stall. We shoveled all
the hay and other stuff onto a pile in the barnyard. Was
that a dirty job! I didn't blame the cow for wanting to
get out.

After that we had to get the eggs and then go to the garden and pick beans again. I couldn't see why the beans couldn't wait, but the Eggman said, We have to take them to town.

I asked, You mean the city?

He said, No, the village.

So we carried the beans and tomatoes and eggs out to the truck, and got in ourselves, and the truck wouldn't go!

Well, he swore like anything, and stamped his foot on the gas pedal and turned the key, but it wouldn't go. He got out and lifted the hood and looked inside, and said, Somebody's been monkeying with this thing.

Then he looked at me and said, Did you touch it?

I was so surprised I couldn't answer at first, but then I said, Me? I never went near it.

He said, It'll take me all morning to find out what's wrong. Something the matter with the wiring.

I asked him, What are you going to do?

He said, How do I know? You sure do ask dumb questions.

So I didn't ask any more. After a while he said, Have to get the neighbor to take this stuff to town. It'll spoil if I don't. Besides, we got no food in the house.

I said, I don't guess they'll mind.

He shouted at me, *I* mind. I don't ask no favors and I don't do none.

Then he calmed down and said, Okay. You walk down the hill to Mrs. Paxson's and tell her my truck is broke down and would she take my stuff to the store for me and get us some groceries. And hurry up, before she leaves herself.

I asked, Where do I go?

He said, Just down the hill. It's the only other house on this road. Now get going. And don't say anything about my back.

I asked, Why not?

He yelled, Because it's none of her business!

I went down the hill till I got to the neighbor's. The house looked a little better than the Eggman's, but not much. There were some toys lying around in the yard, a wagon and pails and shovels, so I knew there were kids there.

I thought, Gee! Kids! Maybe there's somebody to talk to!

A girl came to the door. She was skinny, with jeans and straggly hair, about my age. She said, Who are you?

I said, I come from up the hill.

She said, Oh, from Mike. You staying with him?

Then she called out, Aunt Sadie!

A woman called, Who is it, Noreen? Then she came out. She was as fat as the girl was skinny. I told her what the Eggman wanted, and she said, Okay, tell him we'll be up in a while and get his stuff. What's your name?

I told her Donald Walker, and she asked me a bunch of questions like, Are you any kin to Mike? How long are you staying? Where do you come from? Where's your mother?

Two boys came to the door and stood behind her staring at me. They were younger than me, and they whispered something and laughed to each other.

I said, What's funny? The girl looked at them and told them to keep quiet.

The woman went back inside and I heard her yelling at the kids. I went back to the Eggman's place, and pretty soon she came in her car, a beat-up old white station wagon, and backed into the driveway. The kids were in the back, leaning out and making faces.

She put Mike's stuff in her car, and Mike gave her a list of things he wanted. She got in the car, yelled at the kids to sit down, and drove off. Mike didn't say thanks or anything. I couldn't understand why he acted so mean.

He started to work on his truck but pretty soon his back hurt too much and he went to the house and sat on the porch. He looked miserable.

I asked him, You want me to do something?

He shook his head. Then he said, I got to do a job, but it's pretty dirty. You wouldn't like it.

I said, I don't mind. (I didn't know what it was.)

He said, Okay, come on. And he got up and hobbled out to the chicken house. I went, too.

Well, gosh! If there's a dirtier job than cleaning out a chicken house I don't know what it is. It was awful. We scraped stuff off the nests and off the floor. Dust and feathers and chicken manure were all over us, me especially. I did most of the work because Mike's back hurt him too much.

I thought, I'll never like chicken again after this. I shoveled the stuff out and put it in a pile, and did it smell! I don't think there is anything that smells worse.

Mike said, This stuff is good for the garden. I thought, If this is what you have to do to have a garden, forget it.

As we were going out of the chicken yard, the gate swung loose. One hinge was gone.

Mike said, Doggone it, I got to fix that when my back gets better.

I said, Do you want me to fix it?

He said, No. I'll do it myself. Right now I'll tie it up.

He tied it with a piece of rope. Then we went back to the house.

I never was so dirty in my life. I was covered with dust and I itched like crazy. I got a bucket of water and washed myself the best I could. The only trouble was, I didn't have any clean clothes.

So the Eggman said, In that room upstairs there are some things, you can probably wear them.

I went up and looked. In the closet I found some overalls and a shirt. They were too big, but I rolled up the arms and legs. I put them on and went down, and he was sitting looking miserable again.

I asked him, Whose clothes are those?

He answered, They used to belong to my boy.

I didn't know he had a boy, so I asked, Where is he?

He said, He grew up and went away. I don't know where he is.

Then he got up and went in the bedroom and lay down.

I thought, Just my luck, he had a kid but he's grown up. That's mean, for a son to go away and leave his father. If I had a father I sure would stick with him.

All of a sudden I remembered my own family, my mother and the kids and my brother John. I wondered what they were doing.

Well, we had some lunch, not much, because there was almost no food in the house. After a while I heard a rattling noise and looked out. There was that girl, dragging a kid's wagon.

She said, Hi, I brought your stuff.

Mike came into the kitchen and sat down. The girl and I unloaded the groceries and she gave him the change that was left from trading the eggs and vegetables and buying the food. Then she looked at him and said, You sick?

He said, No, I'm not sick. What gave you that idea?

She said, My aunt says you look sick.

Mike said, Well, I'm not, and you can tell that to your aunt.

She said, My aunt says you shouldn't be living here by yourself.

He said, Okay, go on home now. Thanks for bringing the stuff.

She said, Can I look at the calf?

Mike looked around sharp at that. He said, How'd you know the calf came?

She said, The boys were playing in the field and saw it.

He said, You tell those kids to stay out of my place, hear? Or they'll be sorry.

She said, Okay, but I want to see the calf.

Mike said to me, You go with her, show her where it is.

So I went, but she seemed to know where to go without me telling her. We went to the field, and the cow was standing in the brook, drinking. The calf was resting under the tree. When it saw us, it got up and kicked up its hind legs and began to run. Then it came back and stood beside its mother. Noreen went over and patted it and scratched its head.

She said, It's a nice calf. Good thing it's a heifer, not a bull calf.

I asked her why, and she said, Bull calves go right to the butcher, but a heifer will give milk, so she's worth keeping, or maybe Mike will sell her to some farmer. I hope he doesn't, then maybe I can have her some day.

I couldn't understand her. I said, How could you have her?

She said, My aunt says Mike is getting too old to stay here by himself. She says he should be in the County Home, and when he goes, she'll buy the place.

When I heard that I was pretty surprised. Suddenly I thought, Boy, she has a nerve saying that. It's *his* business!

I felt like saying it out loud, but then I thought it really wasn't my business. But I felt mad just the same. I remembered his saying, Don't tell her about my back, and I began to catch on to what he meant.

I asked, Why does she want to buy the place?

Noreen said, So she can board more kids. His place is bigger than hers.

I said, Board more kids? What do you mean?

And she said, Oh, those kids that live with us are welfare kids. The state pays for them. I have to help take care of them, though. I wish I didn't. They're a pain in the neck.

I said, I thought they were your brothers.

She shook her head. If they were, I'd make them behave. I wish my aunt would smack them once in a while, but she doesn't. She's afraid they'll tell the social worker.

I said, What do they do that's so bad? They're pretty young.

She said, You don't know them. They're mean.

I asked her, Do you live here all the time?

She said, Yes, my mother died so I stay with my aunt. I don't mind in winter when I can go to school, but in summer I have to help all the time. Come on, let's find the kittens.

I wondered how she knew about the kittens. She said, Oh, we come up here every week when Mike is away.

I knew Mike wouldn't like that. I wondered if I should tell him.

We went to the barn and Noreen climbed up and came down with the kittens. She seemed to know just where to find them. They sure were cute, with little round faces and pointy ears and tails. She sat down on the barn floor and played with them.

When she was playing with the kittens, or patting the calf, she looked different, somehow. Her face looked nicer. When she talked about her aunt or the kids she looked mean. I didn't blame her. It's no fun to mind kids all the time. Only Julie and Douglas never do anything *bad*.

After a while she said, Well, I better go or Aunt Sadie will skin me. I sneaked out without the boys and

that means she has to mind them. I wish I could take
one of the kittens, I bet Mike wouldn't mind, but the
boys would pester it to death.

We started back to the house. On the way I thought
of something.

I said, Mike told me he had a son. Why doesn't he
come and take care of the place for him?

She laughed and said, Oh, Aunt Sadie says his son
isn't ever coming back. She says he's in jail or some
place.

She took her wagon and walked off down the hill.

four

We had hamburgers and rolls for supper, and cake and canned peaches, and I got some corn from the garden. It sure was good. We had milk to drink, too.

I asked Mike why we had to buy milk if he had a cow, and he said the first few days after a calf was born the milk was no good for people to drink. But pretty soon he'd start milking.

Maybe tomorrow, he said, if I can bend over.

But the next day he wasn't any better. I did the chores myself. I didn't have to bother about the cow, she was okay, but I fed the chickens and got the eggs.

Then I made breakfast. I managed to light the stove all right, and I made coffee and fried eggs and bacon. We had cereal and milk and bread and butter and peaches. It's funny how much better you feel if you have something decent to eat.

In the afternoon Mike went out to try to fix the truck. He poked around inside the hood, and then he said, I just can't figure it. She was all right Wednesday night. Looks like somebody pulled a wire out. Funny. I didn't see anybody around here, did you?

I said, No, nobody but Noreen.

Of course the truck was out by the road. You wouldn't see it if you were in the bedroom or out in the field.

Mike said, I have to get a special pair of pliers to fix her. Must have some in the cellar. Maybe tomorrow I'll look around and see if I can find them.

I said, You want me to look?

He said, No, never mind. I think I'll just rest a little. And he sat down in his chair on the porch.

I didn't know what to do. I hoped he would get that truck fixed. If he didn't, how could I get home? But as long as he felt so bad, how could he fix it?

I said to him, Mike, maybe you should have a doctor for your back.

Well, he nearly hit the ceiling. He twisted around in his chair and yelled at me, Doctor! What do I want with a doctor? All they can do is cart you off to the hospital or stick you in a home. Might as well be dead.

I said, Well, gee, I didn't mean anything. I'm sorry.

But he shouted at me, Go on, do something useful instead of standing there staring at me.

So I walked around the back of the house and sat down on the back step. Blackie came and sat down beside me and I thought, Why can't people be as nice as animals?

I scratched his ears and he licked my face to show
he liked me. Then suddenly he stiffened up. He growled
and the hair on his back stood up.

I said, Hey, what's the matter with you? What did
I do?

But it wasn't me he was growling at. He was looking
toward the barn. He must have seen something move.
He started walking. I got up and went, too.

I said, What's over there? But he just kept on walking. We got to the barn and I looked inside. It was dark
in there and I couldn't see at first. Blackie walked to one
of the stalls and growled again.

Then I heard a faint sound. *Meow!* And then I heard
a giggle.

I called out, Who's there?

Nobody answered, but I heard that *meow* again.

I went to the stall and there were those two boys from Paxsons'. They had hold of the kittens. The bigger kid was holding a kitten up by the tail and it was yelling. They had the other one in a plastic bag.

I shouted, Hey, what are you doing?

The bigger one said, Noreen thinks we don't know where these cats are. We'll show her.

I tried to grab the kitten away from him but he dumped it in the bag and ran past me.

I yelled, Hey! Stop! Let go of those cats!

He yelled back, They're not your cats, you don't live here.

I ran after him and he threw the bag on the ground and ran off, but Blackie jumped on him. He didn't hurt him, but he scared him and the boy started to yell.

I grabbed the bag and let the kittens out. They scooted back in the barn. The other kid wanted to jump on me but he was afraid of Blackie. So he stood and shouted, You leave my brother alone! You made the dog bite him! I'll tell on you!

I said, The dog didn't hurt him, now you both get out of here before I give you a good licking.

The little one said, You try and hit us! We'll get even with you and Mike, too!

Suddenly I thought of something. I said, Did you leave the gate open and let the cow out? Did you fool with the truck?

The big one said, Wouldn't you like to know?

He picked up a stone and threw it at me, and they both ran away.

I thought, I'll have to tell Mike. I didn't like to make him feel worse, but he had to know. Anyhow, I was so mad myself I had to tell somebody.

I went to the porch where he was sitting and I said, Mike, you know those kids from Paxsons'? I caught them in the barn just now trying to steal the kittens. And you know what? I bet they're the ones that let the cow out and maybe fooled with the truck while you were sleeping.

After I said it I wished I hadn't. He got so mad that I was scared. His face got all red and he banged his fist on the chair and shouted, Damn it! and even worse things.

He yelled, I knew it was something like that. I'd like to get my hands on those little rats.

I said, Well, Blackie and I chased them and I think we scared them.

He calmed down a little and said, It's not the first time. Those kids are no good. It's not their fault. They have no bringing up. That woman just keeps them for the board money she gets. The girl isn't bad.

I said, I'll keep watch so they don't come back.

But suddenly he wasn't mad any more. He just looked all stooped over and old. Then he said, No, Donald, you can't do that. (It was the first time he said my name.) I've been thinking about what to do. I was just going to tell you when you started talking about the kids. Tomorrow you go down and ask Mrs. Paxson to phone the TV man in the village. He drives to the city about once a week. You could go with him. Then you phone your folks and tell them you're coming.

I said, But why don't I wait till Wednesday and go with you?

He shook his head. No. I can't fix that truck. It's ready for the junk pile. And I guess I am, too. Let's face it. That woman wants this place, might as well let her have it.

I hollered, No! You can't!

He said, I thought I'd keep it for my son, if he ever came back, but looks like he's not coming.

I said, Wait! Maybe he is. You don't know. Maybe he's on his way here now. Your back will be okay, you'll be able to fix the truck.

But he just shook his head and said, No, it's the junk pile, for me and the truck.

I couldn't stand to see him like that. I thought I'd rather have him yelling at me.

I went out and walked to the field. The cow was lying under the tree chewing, and the calf was lying beside her, and a few birds were flying around in the sky. The sun had gone down and the sky was all pink around the edges, and sort of greenish-blue up above. It was so peaceful. I hated the idea of those people coming in and spoiling everything.

But what could I do about it? It was the Eggman's business, after all. It wasn't up to me.

The next morning the Eggman said, Okay, now you go down to Paxsons' and phone.

He told me again to tell Mrs. Paxson to find out when the TV man was going to the city. He said, It's Sunday, so tell her to call him at home, not in the shop. Go on, now.

All the way down the hill I kept thinking, It's not fair. A thing doesn't have to be thrown on the junk pile just because it's old. You can put in a new part. A person doesn't have to be thrown away either. Suddenly I remembered Aunt Lizzie telling Mom, Sarah, just because I'm old doesn't mean I'm ready for the junk pile. I could see what she meant.

I didn't want to go to Paxsons'. I hated them. I could see the house ahead of me and I hoped they weren't home. I thought, I won't go in there.

I couldn't stand the idea of those kids listening while I explained about Mike. But what could I do? Who could I get to help?

All of a sudden I knew. I sneaked past the house and started to run. I ran all the way down to the main road. Then I turned left and walked along the road. I walked about a mile and then I saw the gas station.

I thought, Gee, I hope it's open. It's Sunday, maybe it's closed.

But it was open. The man was in there drinking coffee. He said, Good morning, haven't I seen you before?

I said, Yes, I came with Mike last Wednesday. (I could hardly believe that this was only Sunday. It seemed as if a year had passed.) I said, I need to phone my folks. Would you help me?

I gave him the number and said to ask for John.

I thought, Even if he hates me, I have to talk to him.

The man got the operator and said, I want to make a collect call to Mr. John Walker. In a minute he handed me the phone.

John must have been asleep. He said, Hello! Who is this?

I said, It's me, Donald.

He said, Donald! Hi, how are you? Are you okay?

He sounded friendly.

I thought, Gee, maybe he doesn't hate me any more.

So I told him, Listen, John, I need you. Can you come up here? I mean right now.

That must have scared him, because he said, Are you sick? What happened?

I said, No, I'm all right. It's the Eggman.

Then I explained all about it, about the truck, and all. I said, Somebody has to help, and you're the only one I know. You have to get out here some way. Maybe you can take a train or something.

John said, But, Donald, I'd have to find out how to get there.

I said, Wait. And I put the gas station man on. He told John where we were and how to go.

Then I talked again and John said, Okay, I'll figure out some way to get there. Tuesday is my day off but maybe I can swap and get Monday instead. I'll see what the deal is. But, Donald, I don't know what *I* can do.

I said, Well, just come. If you'll come that will be a help.

He said good-bye, and I thanked the man and was going, when he said, Wait a minute. I didn't know Mike was sick. Why didn't you let me know?

I said Mike didn't want anybody to know, and he muttered, Stubborn old fool. Tell him Bill was asking for him.

I started back. It took longer because it was uphill a lot of the way. But at last I got there.

The Eggman asked me, Well, did you fix it up?

I said, Yes, but not today. Tomorrow afternoon.

He said, Okay, I don't mind having you around another day.

I thought I would explode keeping it to myself the rest of the day. I went out to the field with the dog and talked to him. A dog is a good person to talk to, because he'll keep his mouth shut and not spill the beans.

The next day I had to keep busy so I wouldn't have to answer any questions. I washed the dishes. I went to the garden and pulled weeds, and then I picked some more beans and went back to the house and started to fix them for lunch. Suddenly I heard a car coming.

It was a blue Ford. The Eggman looked out and said, Who's that? I don't know that car. It's not the TV man.

I ran out. The car stopped and a man got out. It was John. I ran and hugged him so hard I almost knocked him down. He hugged me, too, and punched me, and I dragged him inside the house and said, It's my brother.

The Eggman was so surprised he couldn't say a word except, Huh! What's the idea?

Then he looked at me and said, So you double-crossed me!

I told him I hadn't said a word except, Tomorrow afternoon. And he admitted that was so.

I asked John where he got the car and he said he borrowed it from his boss. So I showed him the truck and he looked it over and got out his toolbox and got busy fixing it. He said some wires were disconnected, and it needed a new fan belt, but maybe he could tighten the old one for now.

Then I took him all around, showed him the barn and the chicken house and the garden.

After that we went out to the field and sat down. I told him everything that had happened, and he listened. It felt good talking to him again. We were sitting by the brook, watching the water run over the stones, and the cow eating grass, and the calf butting its mother with its head.

I said, I like it here. I feel as if I belong here. I was hoping you'd like it, too.

He said, Yes, I like it.

I said, Hey, you know what? I wish we could stay here. All of us.

As soon as that was out of my mouth I started to get excited. I said, We could live with the Eggman. He's got lots of room, and we could help with the work. What about it?

John said, Wait a minute. He hasn't invited us.

I said, Well, I bet he'd like it. Come on, let's ask him.

He started to laugh and said, Come on, kid, let's be realistic. We can't stay in the Eggman's house. Besides, how would we make a living? I'm no farmer. I'm a city man.

I said, Okay, go ahead and laugh. I guess Mike will have to sell the place and go to the County Home and be dead in a couple of months.

And I walked away. I didn't want John to see my face. But he came after me and said, Wait a minute. Don't get sore. Maybe we can work something out.

So we went back to the house and John talked to the Eggman. He asked him a lot of questions.

I went out to feed the chickens and get the eggs, and when I came back John said, Come here, Donald. I told Mike I have to go back to the city, but I'll come back next Sunday. I'll work on his truck and see if I can get it running. You want to come home with me and then come out again next week?

I said, Okay. Then I had another idea. I said, Wait! Couldn't I stay here? I mean, if Mike wants me to. Then I'll go home when you come next week.

John said, Okay, if Mike wants you.

Mike said, Sure, why not? I can use him. Somebody showed him how to wash dishes.

John laughed and said, Aunt Lizzie.

So we had supper and John went home. After he left, I was cleaning up, when we heard a car coming.

Mike said, Who's that? More company? I ain't had so much company since my wife died ten years ago.

It was the man from the gas station.

He came over and said, Mike, I hear you're enjoying poor health. Why didn't you tell me, you old so-and-so?

Mike said, Bill, you know I don't ask no favors.

But he didn't sound as if he minded Bill coming.

Bill said, I brought some beer, and Coke for the kid. Mind if I sit down for a while?

So we sat on the porch and drank. Then Bill allowed as how he could use some tomatoes, so I went to the garden to get them. He came along and said to me, You staying here?

I said, Just till next week when my brother comes back.

He said, Let me know if you need anything. That old coot is so independent he wouldn't ask for a thing. But he's pretty old, must be seventy or more.

After Bill went away, Mike looked around and said, This place is a mess. When I feel a little better we'll get it fixed up.

I thought, Boy, he sounds better already.

The next week John came back. He brought some

pie and bread that Aunt Lizzie had made. I thought it was pretty nice of her to do that.

John and I went for a walk and talked. He said everybody was fine, Aunt Lizzie was taking care of the kids and they were good. Mom was worried about me, but John told her that I was all right, and she said I could stay longer if the Eggman wanted me, and if I wanted to. John had even brought some clothes in case I stayed.

I said, Do I *want* to! You bet I do! Come on, let's tell him.

But John said, Hold your horses, that's not the way to do it.

And he went and talked to Mike to find out how he felt.

The way it turned out, I stayed all summer. Mike got better and we fixed things, and did the farm work, and sometimes we went to the village.

Finally John drove up to get me, and I was real glad to see him, only when we were leaving and I looked back and saw Blackie and the Eggman standing there watching us go, well, if I had been a little kid I would have bawled. But when we got back I was real glad to see everybody, even Aunt Lizzie.

Now I'm home. It's winter and the Eggman is all alone again. He doesn't drive to the city any more. But he's okay for now. Bill, the gas station man, calls us sometimes so we know. He's got the cow and he's keeping the heifer, and next spring he's going to teach me how to milk, and how to plant the garden.

When I think about the farm, it's not like the picture in the book. It isn't so pretty. The house isn't white, with flowers around it, and there aren't a lot of people smiling. It's poor, and there's dirt and hard work. But it's better than a picture. It's real.

ELEANOR CLYMER has written many books for young people, including *The House on the Mountain* and *We Lived in the Almont*. *Me and the Eggman* stems from two experiences in Mrs. Clymer's life. "When we lived in the city, an old man came to the door once a week with a basket of eggs. He came in a shabby truck and by the time he got to our apartment he usually didn't have much left." Although his eggs weren't very fresh, "I took them, because he was so old and tired." And then, "one summer I stayed at a small farm that took a few boarders. There was a boy staying at the farm who followed the farmer around all day. When it was time to leave, he didn't want to go." Mrs. Clymer adds: "The main point of the story is actually conservation, of people as well as places. People, young and old, have strength and want to be needed; the land has usefulness, too; it's wrong to just throw them away."

DAVID K. STONE grew up in an Oregon town, but remembers vividly his five years on a farm, where he drove a truck and worked in the dairy. He even recalls the first time a hen flew in his face while he was cleaning out the chicken house. Like Donald, he discovered that farming was hard work. And across the street was an old man who appeared to be very grumpy, but who was kind underneath his leathery surface, much like the Eggman. Mr. Stone has used pencil and wash for his illustrations, evoking a mood close to his own life experience.

The display type is set in Century Schoolbook and the text type is set in Janson. The book is printed by offset.